Shaggy Dogs & Spotty Dogs
& Shaggy & Spotty Dogs

Shaggy Dogs & Spotty Dogs & Shaggy & Spotty Dogs

Written and illustrated by Seymour Leichman

Harcourt Brace Jovanovich, Inc., New York

Library of Congress Cataloging in Publication Data
Leichman, Seymour.
    Shaggy dogs & spotty dogs & shaggy & spotty dogs.
    SUMMARY: Describes "dogs that sing unlikely notes
and dogs who wear plaid overcoats" and many other kinds
of dogs.
    [1. Dogs—Stories.   2. Stories in rhyme]   I. Title.
PZ8.3.L532Sh   [E]   73-75322
ISBN 0-15-278020-3

For Sam

There are shaggy dogs

and spotty dogs

and shaggy
and spotty dogs…

scruffy pups

and fluffy pups

and scruffy fluffy puffy pups...

frisky dogs and lazy dogs,

risky dogs
and crazy dogs,

and snoopy dogs
and snoozy dogs

and snoopy snoozy droopy dogs...

thin ones,
tall ones,

big ones,
small ones...

lost ones,

found ones,

upside-down ones,

and chase-their-tails-all-around ones.

There are dogs with studded collars made in leather

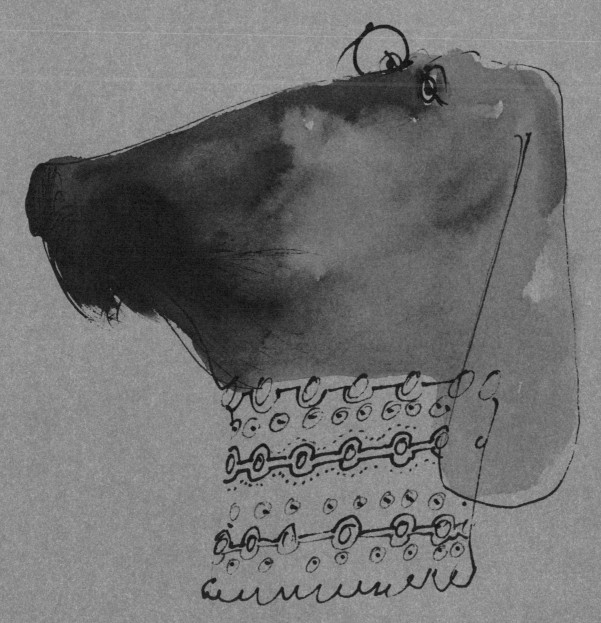

and dogs that look peculiar all together.

There are dogs
that win a ribbon every year.

Some dogs are even truly fond of beer.

Dogs that sing unlikely notes
and that wear plaid overcoats.

There are even dogs I know
that wear galoshes in the snow.

Dogs named Bo
and dogs named Clyde
who have enormous bones to hide.

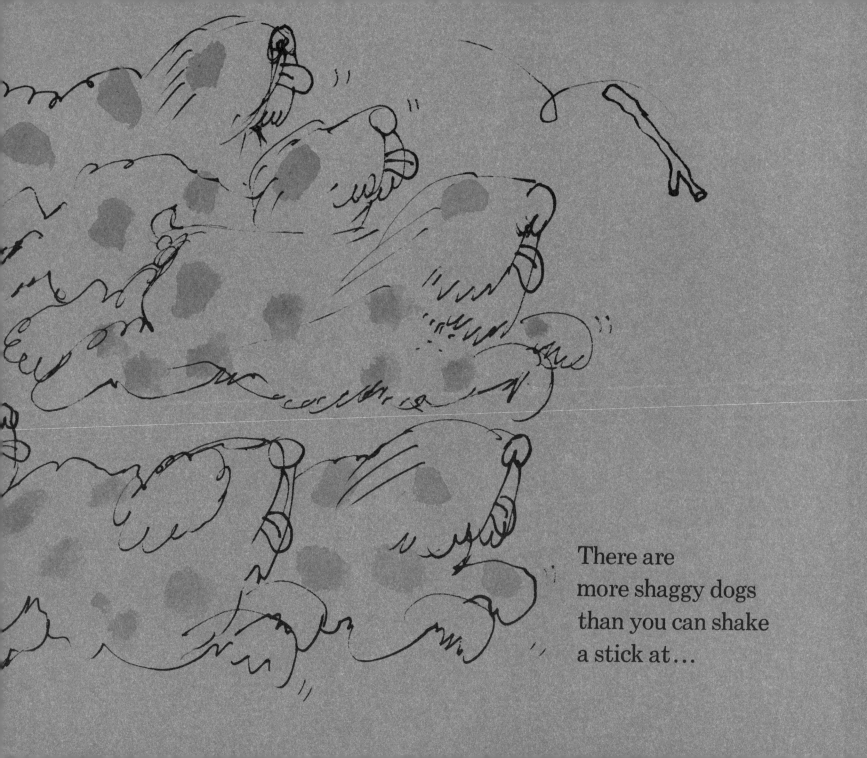

There are
more shaggy dogs
than you can shake
a stick at...

who love a salty hand
that they can take a lick at.

So dream sweet dreams,
your dog is near
to guard you through the night.
Who ever said,
"He's man's best friend,"
was absolutely right.